THE
How to Catch
a Mermaid and
Unicorn
ACTIVITY BOOK
for KIDS

SOURCEBOOKS
wonderland

COLOR THE PAGE AND READ THE RHYME FOR EXTRA FUN!

Our favorite thing to do at the beach is jog, can you find our loyal dog?

CAN YOU CATCH SIGHT OF THESE HIDDEN PICTURES!$?

- [ ] **A BOOK**
- [ ] **THREE YELLOW EGGS**
- [ ] **A BLUE RIBBON**
- [ ] **A STARFISH**
- [ ] **A TIARA**
- [ ] **TWO BOOTS**

CAN YOU CATCH SIGHT OF THESE HIDDEN PICTURES?

- [ ] A PUPPY SNOUT
- [ ] A GREEN MARBLE
- [ ] A MUSHROOM
- [ ] PAINTBRUSH WITH ORANGE PAINT
- [ ] THREE FROSTED CUPCAKES
- [ ] AN ALLIGATOR

FOLLOW THESE FUN STEPS AND LEARN HOW TO DRAW!

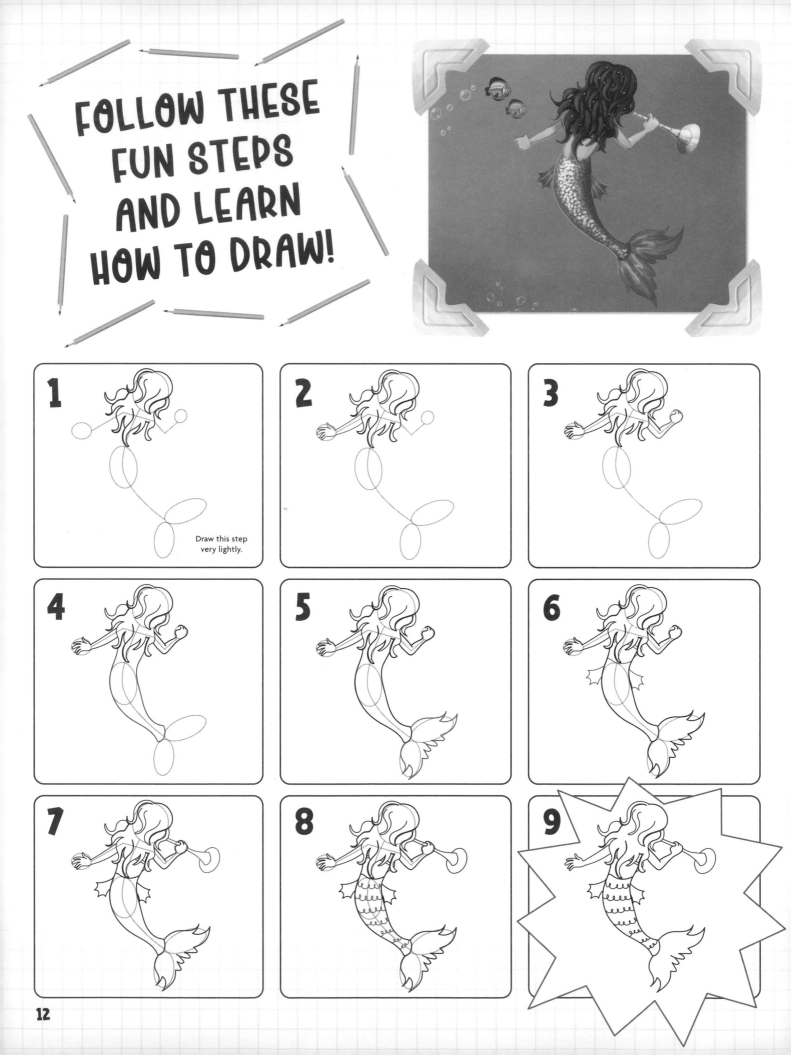

1 Draw this step very lightly.

2

3

4

5

6

7

8

9

FOLLOW THESE FUN STEPS AND LEARN HOW TO DRAW!

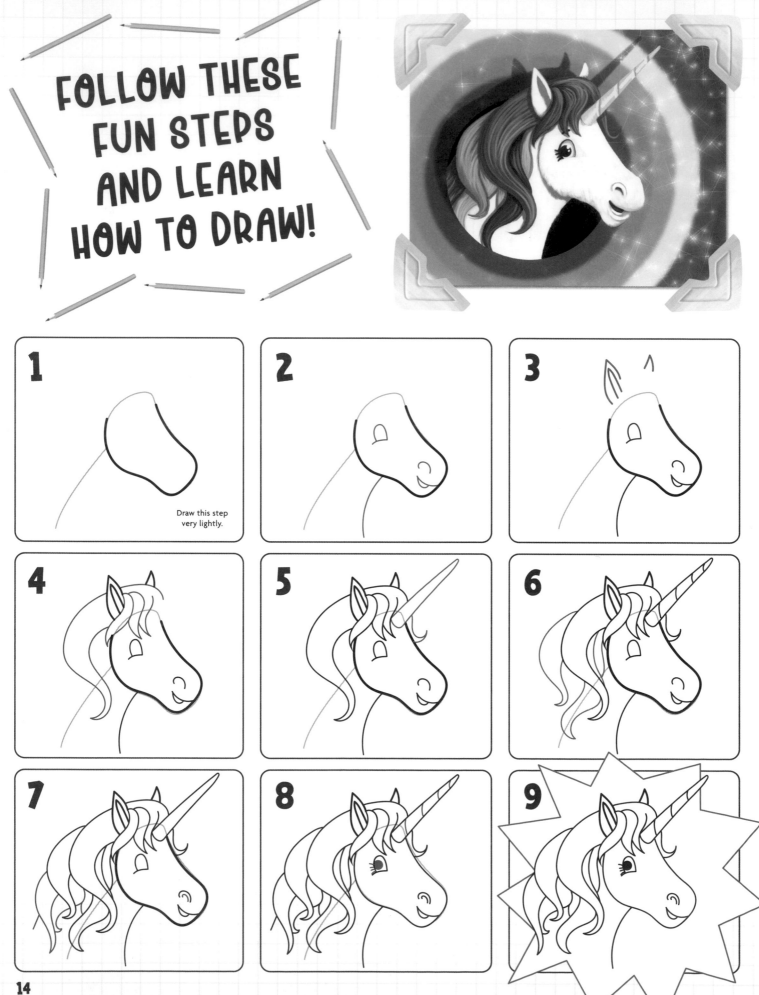

1

Draw this step very lightly.

2

3

4

5

6

7

8

9

To catch a mermaid
in your trap,
use something
that can snap!

CONNECT THE DOTS TO REVEAL A TRAP!

To trap a unicorn you'll have to be smart to win,

try using a beautiful home for it to live in!

CONNECT THE DOTS TO REVEAL A TRAP!

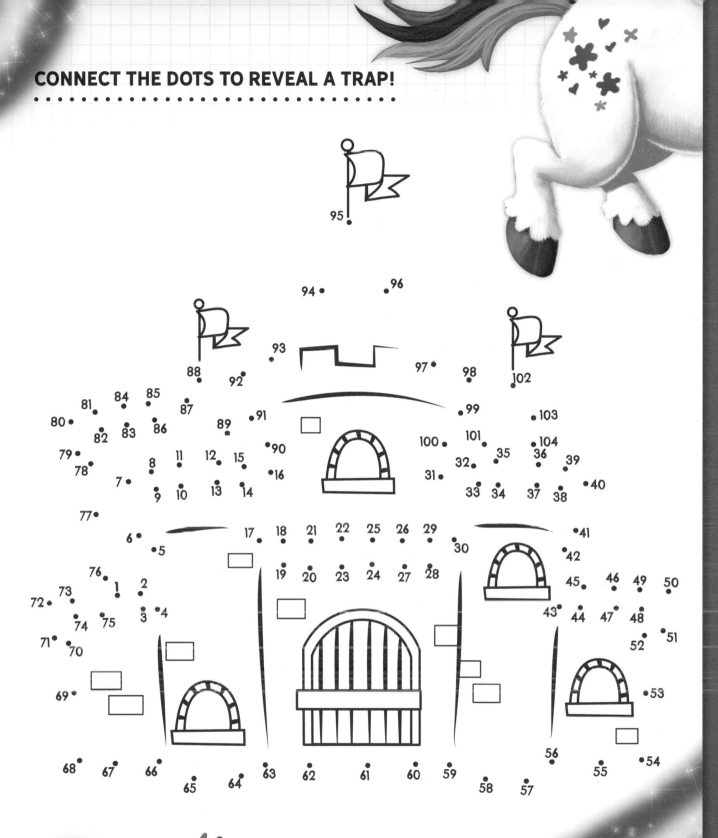

20

COMPLETE THE STORY WITH A FRIEND OR MAKE THE SILLIEST STORY EVER AND SHARE WITH A FRIEND LATER!

Our mermaid comes to save the day!

She made a trap to save us.

She scares the sharks by _____

_____

_____

_____ !

(complete the story)

But *how* to catch a mermaid?

You don't learn this in school.

We'll need to build a _____ trap
(describing word)

and start near the _____ .
(place)

CAN YOU AVOID THE STARS AND RAINBOWS TO HELP THE CATCH CLUB KIDS CATCH THE UNICORN?

COMPLETE THE STORY WITH A FRIEND OR MAKE THE SILLIEST STORY EVER AND SHARE WITH A FRIEND LATER!

The kids think they have spotted me—

I thought I'd blend in here!

I cannot let them catch me

or my magic will _____

_____

_____!

(complete the story)

I dodge the _____ parachute

(describing word)

being launched from down below.

I do a spin and leave a trail

of _____ as I go.

(describing word)

SOMEWHERE OVER THE MAGIC RAINBOW

Try this fun activity to help you catch a unicorn!

DIFFICULTY:

MATERIALS

- Hot glue gun*
- Glue stick
- Scissors*
- Box lid
- Glittery construction paper in rainbow colors (or make your own in Step 1)
- Cotton balls
- Marshmallow cereal (or other rainbow cereal)
- Craft stick (or other device to prop up box lid)

   Requires parental supervision

STEAM CONNECTION

Time to put your engineering caps on! This trap uses a craft stick to prop up the lid that will catch our unicorn when it shrinks in size, and it's up to you to figure out which angle works best for the stick and lid. Experiment with the angle of the stick and where you position it against the lid to see which option will hold up the longest and snatch the unicorn the quickest!

DIRECTIONS

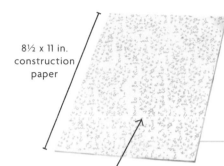

8½ x 11 in. construction paper

1-in. border   Gold glitter

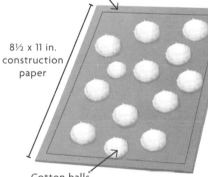

8½ x 11 in. construction paper

Cotton balls

1 **GLITTER ALERT!** If you already have glitter construction paper, this will be used for your cut-out gold coins later on. If you don't have glitter paper already, spread glue all over construction paper and sprinkle with gold glitter. Shake off excess and let dry.

2 Grab your glue stick again! This time, spread glue on another piece of paper and stick cotton balls all over it, leaving a 1-inch border.

3 Cut 5 x 1 in. strips of construction paper to create a rainbow path. Glue each colored strip to the top border of the cotton-ball paper.

5 x 1 in. strips of construction paper

Cereal and
marshmallow
nuggets

4 Sprinkle marshmallow cereal nuggets on top of the cotton balls. (Your unicorn won't be able to resist this rainbow-cloud path to sugary goodness!)

8½ x 11 in. glitter paper from step 1

5 With adult supervision, cut out coins from your glitter paper to add to your cloud in the next step.

Circles in shape of gold coins

DID YOU KNOW?

A rainbow is formed by light reflecting off raindrops! Raindrops act like a prism when they are in the air. When light enters a water droplet, it bounces off the back of the water droplet and reflects at angles, causing the light to bend. This process allows you to see different colors!

6 Wrap the box lid in colored construction paper. Prop up the lid with a craft stick (with its other end on the cotton-ball cloud) to create a **SNAPPITY SNAP TRAP** when your devious little unicorn tries to eat its marshmallows!

Shoebox lid

Craft stick

HIDDEN PICTURE SOLUTIONS

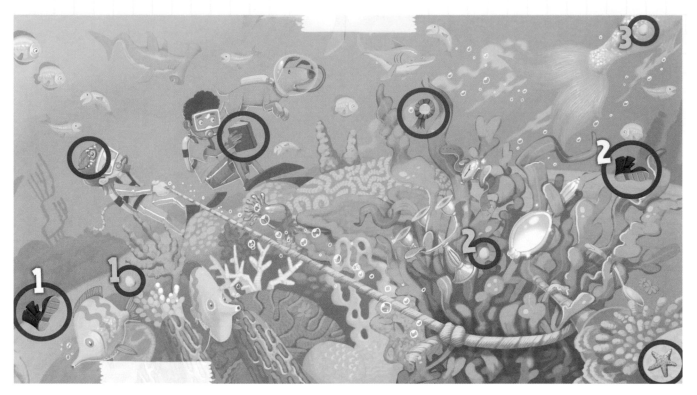

From left to right: boot 1, a tiara, yellow egg 1, a book, a blue ribbon, yellow egg 2, boot 2, yellow egg 3, a starfish

From left to right: an alligator, a mushroom, frosted cupcake 1, a green marble, frosted cupcake 2, paintbrush with orange paint, frosted cupcake 3, a puppy snout

SPOT THE DIFFERENCE SOLUTIONS

From left to right: sock has turned yellow, missing unicorn on shirt, missing net, additional penguin, missing flower on Unicorn

DOT-TO-DOT SOLUTIONS

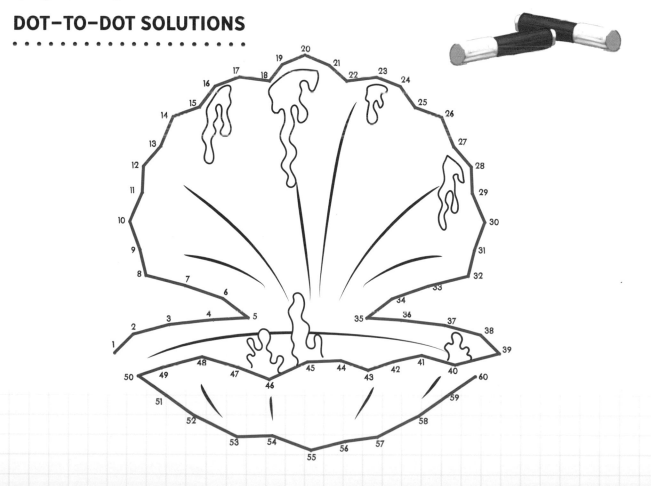

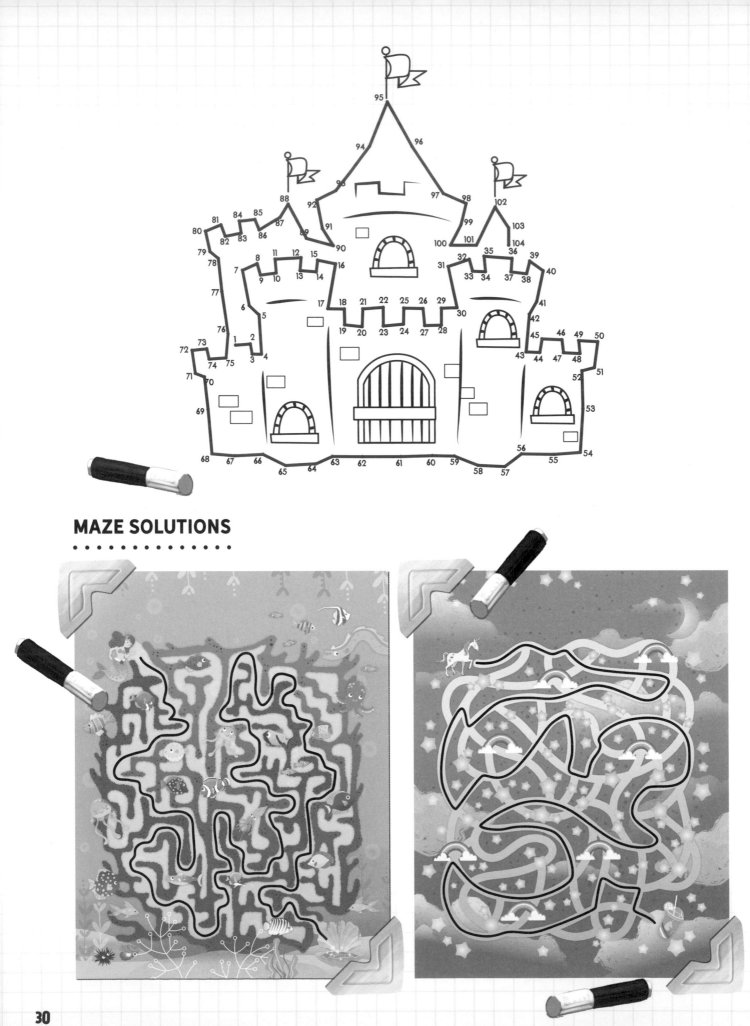

MAZE SOLUTIONS